Adapted by Marilyn Easton
Based on the original screenplay by Elise Allen
Illustrations by Rita Lichtwardt, Carrie Perlow,
Taia Morley, and Christian Musselman

SCHOLASTIC INC.

New York   Toronto   London   Auckland

Sydney   Mexico City   New Delhi   Hong Kong

ISBN 978-0-545-33312-2

12 11 10 9 8 7 6 5 4 3   11 12 13 14 15 16/0

Printed in the U.S.A.   40

First printing, September 2011

Special thanks to Vicki Jaeger, Monica Okazaki, Ann McNeill, Emily Kelly, Sharon Woloszyk, Julia Phelps, Tanya Mann, Rob Hudnut, Tiffany J. Shuttleworth, Gabrielle Miles, Lily Martinez, and Walter P. Martishius.

Chapter 1

It was two days before Christmas and Barbie, Skipper, Stacie, and Chelsea were on a plane heading to New York City to see their aunt Millicent.

Barbie was so excited—she couldn't wait to get there. Not only would she be in New York for Christmas but her favorite aunt also had front-row seats to the closing night of a Broadway show!

Chelsea, Stacie, and Skipper also were thinking about their fun plans. Chelsea

was going to the Central Park Zoo to see the sea lions. She was determined to be one of the special volunteers selected to feed them! Meanwhile, Stacie was planning to go ice-skating at Rockefeller Center. She had bought extra-special skates just for the occasion. And Skipper was getting the once-in-a-lifetime opportunity to podcast the concert her friend Zoe's band was playing. Skipper was also secretly excited because the band was going to play a song she wrote! Even though Skipper hadn't told her sisters about it, she was really looking forward to her song being performed live. It was going to be the perfect Christmas!

Interrupting the girls' thoughts, the airplane captain's voice came over the loudspeaker. "Ladies and gentlemen, this is your captain speaking," his voice boomed. "We have a severe weather system in our flight path that will force us to make an unscheduled landing in Rochester, Minnesota."

"Is that near Manhattan?" Chelsea asked Stacie.

"I don't think so," Stacie replied. "Does that mean we won't get to New York City today?" she asked Barbie.

"If the storm's really bad, we won't get to New York at all," Skipper answered.

Barbie could see the worried looks on her sisters' faces. "We'll get to New York for Christmas, I promise, even if I have to drive us all the way myself," Barbie said, trying to comfort her sisters.

After they landed, Barbie rented a car and started driving carefully through the snowstorm. Skipper was using her GPS to help navigate. But the snow was getting thicker, and it was getting dark out.

"Are we close to New York yet?" Chelsea asked.

"We're not trying to get to New York," Barbie explained. "We just want to get to the nearest big airport where we can catch a plane that will take us to New York." Barbie was determined to get her sisters to New

York so that they could do all of the fun things they had planned, no matter how long it took!

"But we've been in the car for *hours*," Stacie whined.

"And I have to go to the bathroom!" Chelsea added.

"Can't you hold it?" Stacie asked.

"You guys, it's fine. We'll stop here," Barbie said as she spotted an inn in the distance.

Barbie and her sisters pulled into the parking lot of the inn. When they got out of the car, they saw a Christmas wreath on the door and lights glowing inside. Barbie walked up to the door and tried to open it. It was locked. Her heart sank. It was really late—everyone inside was probably already asleep. Barbie hoped that someone would come to the door so that the girls could stay at the inn for the night.

"Oh, let me!" Chelsea said as she ran past Barbie to ring the doorbell. The doorbell sounded like sleigh bells. Suddenly, the door swung open and a woman was standing before them.

"Hello-ho-ho-ho! Welcome to the Tannenbaum Inn. My name's Christie Clauson, and I am at your service!" she cheered.

"Hi! We saw the vacancy sign. I hope it's not too late—" Barbie said as a wave of relief washed over her.

"Too late? But you're right on time!" Christie said happily. She motioned for the sisters to come inside.

Inside the lodge there was a whirl of activity. The entire lobby was full of holiday decorations. There was an enormous decorated tree in the corner. Several people wearing aprons were putting the finishing touches on the tree. The sisters noticed they were all very short and had pointy ears. Some of them were sitting at a large table wrapping presents, while others were stacking presents in a huge pile. The sisters could not believe their eyes.

"Wow, you really get into the Christmas spirit around here," Barbie said as she looked around the room.

"Oh, you don't know the half of it," Christie said with a wink. "The Elifs and I love to get in the holiday spirit."

"Elves! I knew it! You said your name is Christie *Clauson*, right? And it's the Tannenbaum Inn, like the Christmas song. And you have elves wrapping Christmas presents. This is Santa's workshop!" Chelsea said with excitement.

"Chelsea, we're in Minnesota. Santa's workshop is at the North Pole. Everyone knows that," Stacie said.

Chelsea looked at Stacie. "But the elves . . ." she insisted.

"*Elifs*. The Elif family," Christie explained. "That's their last name. We do a big toy drive every Christmas, and they always help me out. We put everything together and wrap up the gifts, then my uncle swings by on Christmas Eve to pick up and deliver the gifts."

"But the Elifs all have pointy ears and they're small," Chelsea said.

"Hello, rude!" Stacie said as she rolled her eyes. "So embarrassing!"

One of the Elifs came up to the girls. "It's okay. She's right. We are small." The Elif looked at Chelsea and smiled kindly. "But small people can do big things, right, Chelsea? As for the pointy ears . . ." She trailed off as she pulled off one of her pointy ears and put it on Chelsea's ear. The Elif then spoke into a pin on her collar that was shaped like a sprig of holly.

Chelsea heard exactly what the Elif was saying, as if she were talking right into Chelsea's ear. Chelsea laughed as she realized that the pointy ears were actually headsets. But then she looked upset. "So this isn't Santa's workshop?"

"Sure it is!" Christie replied. "Any place where people come together to bring Christmas to others is one of Santa's workshops, don't you think?"

"I guess so," Chelsea said.

"But hey, it's getting late and you all must be tired. I'll show you to your room," Christie said. "You're welcome to stay as long as you like. It's always fun having company for the holidays."

"Thanks," Barbie replied. "But we're only here until morning. We are going to catch the first flight from Minneapolis to New York. We have big plans for Christmas," she said, looking at her sisters.

"Then let's get you all rested up so you can make the most of them!" Christie responded. She turned to two Elifs. "Cole, Ivy, bring them to the best room in the house!" And at that, Cole and Ivy piled the sisters' suitcases into one tall stack and led the girls to their room.

Chapter 2

Once they were inside their room, the sisters looked around. The beautiful room had four sleigh beds along the wall. Even though the girls were tired, the excitement of the past few minutes made them feel wide awake. Stacie bounced a soccer ball on her knee while Chelsea held a dress-up outfit and danced in the mirror as she sang to herself. Skipper was busy updating her blog, which she wrote as "P. J. Sherwood," a name she made up.

Barbie called their aunt Millicent. "We miss you, too!" Barbie said. "Yep, Skipper's booking us on a morning flight. We'll call you from the gate. See you soon! Bye!"

Barbie turned to her sisters as she hung up the phone. "Aunt Millie sends her love."

"Did she say she's excited for the sea lion show?" Chelsea asked.

"Did she say how much snow is on the ground? Did she say if it's enough to snowshoe?" asked Stacie.

"Did she say she's sorry she won't see us this trip?" Skipper added sarcastically.

"What? What do you mean?" Stacie asked.

"I mean there's another storm coming tonight," Skipper said as she looked at her computer screen. "Major flight cancellations are expected throughout the

Midwest. There's no way our plane is taking off tomorrow."

"But it has to," Stacie said with a frown, not wanting to believe her sister. "We have to get to New York for the perfect Christmas."

"I think we have to kiss the perfect Christmas good-bye," Skipper said with disappointment.

"But Barbie *promised*. She said we'd get to New York for Christmas. Right, Barbie?" Chelsea asked, looking at her sister with wide, hopeful eyes.

Barbie didn't know what to do. She didn't want to lie, but she also didn't want to upset her sisters even more. She paused. "You know what? Weather reports are wrong all the time. Our flight is first thing in the morning. I bet we can get out and be in New

York City before the storm even starts."

"Really? You think there's a chance I could still make Zoe's show tomorrow night?" Skipper asked hopefully.

"And I can skate at Rockefeller Center?" Stacie asked.

"And I'll feed the sea lions?" Chelsea added.

"Yep. And I'll be sitting in the front row at the Broadway show, I'm sure of it," Barbie said with a smile. "I promise, we'll have the perfect Christmas. But first we should get to bed. We have a big day ahead of us tomorrow."

The sisters all climbed into bed and said their good nights. Barbie turned off the light. As she tried to fall asleep, Barbie wished upon a star that she could keep her promise.

Chapter 3

Hours later, Barbie was still no closer to falling asleep. She tiptoed outside their room and headed downstairs. As she walked down the staircase, she heard a beautiful voice softly singing. When Barbie got to the bottom of the stairs, she saw Skipper looking out a window at the snow. Barbie couldn't believe the beautiful voice was from her sister! As she moved closer, Skipper didn't seem to notice.

After Skipper finished her song, Barbie burst into applause.

"Skipper, that was wonderful!" Barbie gushed. "I had no idea you could sing like that!"

Skipper was mortified. "It's nothing, it's just . . . it's nothing."

"Nothing? Skipper, your voice is

beautiful! And the song—I don't think I've ever heard it before. Do you know what it's called? I'd love to download it."

"You can't—it . . . it's something I kind of wrote," Skipper said with a shrug.

Barbie was amazed. "Get out! You wrote that? Skipper! I didn't even know you wrote music. You need to record that. You have to. It's too good not to. And I know tons of people we can get it to. Oh! We're looking for music for my newest movie! What if we can get your song into it? It'll be huge. Then for the next movie maybe you can do all the music—like a big family project!"

"Stop! Can't you just butt out? I'm not a baby! I don't need you to jump in and do everything for me," Skipper said sharply.

"What?" Barbie asked with a look of shock on her face. "I'm not! I don't!"

"You do! You always do. It's why I never told you about my music. I knew you'd take over and try to control everything!" Skipper yelled.

Barbie could not believe how upset her sister was getting. "I don't want to control anything. I just want to help!" she insisted.

"Right, 'cause I couldn't possibly do anything on my own," Skipper concluded.

"That's not what I said at all! Skipper, you're my sister and I want to help you. Why are you acting like it's the most horrible thing in the world?" Barbie asked.

"Because I don't want your help. I want to do this by myself!" Skipper replied.

Barbie could tell that this was really important to Skipper. "Okay. I'm sorry if you feel like I control things for you. I don't mean to. If you don't want my help, I won't help. I promise. It's a really good song, though. You could totally do something with it. On your own, I mean."

"I was going to. Zoe's band was supposed to perform it tomorrow in New York. I was going to podcast it on my P. J. Sherwood blog. I get a lot of hits, so I knew I could really help break the band, and I'd also get my song out there in the coolest way. And I wanted to surprise you, so I kept it a secret. It was a really big deal." Skipper looked out the window at the snow. "But we're not getting to New York, are we?"

Barbie thought for a moment. "Probably not. But even if we can't, the band can still perform your song, right? Maybe they could hire another podcaster, and you could link to it. Then maybe you could use the audio and shoot your own video and post it on—"

Barbie stopped herself, since she could see that Skipper was getting frustrated again. "Sorry. It's a habit."

Skipper let out a sigh. "The song's not ready. I need to sit with them in person and tweak it first. I don't want it out there before it's really ready. It was going to be great, though: awesome band, live audience . . . and they're new, so they don't get a lot of shows. Tomorrow night was going to be the big chance to get my song out there in the perfect way . . . but now it's not going to happen." Skipper paused. "I'm going to go back to bed. Good night."

Barbie watched sadly as Skipper walked up the stairs.

When Barbie woke up the next morning, her sisters were already awake. Chelsea

and Stacie were looking out the window. Skipper was sitting in front of her laptop on her bed.

"Look! The sun's up! It's not snowing anymore!" Chelsea cheered.

"So our plane will take off and we can go to New York!" Stacie added. She took Chelsea's hand and they both climbed on the bed and started jumping. Barbie was really excited, too. She turned to Skipper, but Skipper did not look as happy as her sisters.

"Skipper?" Barbie asked.

Skipper shook her head. "Our flight was canceled."

"Canceled?" Chelsea said with disbelief.

"It snowed most of the night. The runways aren't clear. They'll get us on another flight, but they can't tell us when. With so many flights canceled, it's probably going to be a couple days," Skipper explained.

"But Christmas is tomorrow! I'll miss the special sea lion feeding!" Chelsea said.

Skipper turned to her sister. "We'll miss everything. All of us will."

The sisters were quiet. They wouldn't be able to have the perfect Christmas after all. Barbie wanted to try to make them feel better, even if she was also disappointed.

"We can always go to New York next Christmas. The sea lions will still be there. So will all the ice-skating," Barbie said.

"Some things won't be there next year. Your show won't be playing next year. Zoe's band won't be performing. Plus, Aunt Millie doesn't come to New York every year," Skipper said.

Chelsea gasped. "Barbie, what about Santa? We're not where we're supposed to be. How will Santa know how to find us? How will he get us our presents?"

"Come on, Chelsea. Santa always knows where people are, whether they're at home or not. Right, Barbie?" Stacie said.

"Right," Barbie said with certainty. "But we can help him find us! With our stockings!" Barbie dug through her suitcase and pulled out the decorated stockings. "We'll hang them right here in the room on the windowsill!" she said as she started hanging the stockings. "There. Now Santa will know exactly where to find us—right near the *reindeer*?" she said in shock. Barbie had glanced out the window and thought she saw a herd of reindeer.

"Reindeer? Where? I want to see!" Chelsea said with excitement.

The sisters crowded around the window

to look outside. In the distance, they saw what looked like eight reindeer playing in the snow. Suddenly, one of the reindeer leaped into the air, flying over several of the others before landing.

Chelsea's eyes were open as wide as they could go. "Did you see that? They are reindeer! They're Santa's reindeer! Come on, we have to go see!"

The sisters looked at one another and raced outside.

Chapter 4

The girls were running outside in a snowy field. Christie and a few Elifs were standing together in the distance, laughing and smiling. Christie started walking to the girls. Chelsea was so excited, she almost bumped into her.

Chelsea was barely able to catch her breath. "A reindeer! They're here! Santa's reindeer are here. We saw one flying!" she gasped between breaths.

"Or jumping," Skipper added.

"I believe you. You know why?" Christie said as she leaned into Chelsea. "Because I saw Santa's reindeer, too. They're right here!" Christie motioned for the sisters to follow her. She led them to the crowd of Elfs and a few people from the town. They were watching eight dogs with adorable reindeer antler headbands. The dogs were playing on an agility course and doing tricks. The crowd was amazed.

"Santa's reindeer, at your service! Want to meet them?" Christie asked.

"They're so cute! Are they all your dogs?" Stacie said.

"Oh, no. Every year we pick several dogs from the shelter to play Santa's reindeer and be part of our Canine Christmas. And so far every year all the dogs have been adopted!"

"Can I try taking the dogs through the agility course?" Stacie asked.

"Ooh, me too!" Chelsea added.

Stacie was annoyed. "Can't you do something else?" she asked.

"It's no problem," Christie replied. "We've got lots of dogs. Stacie, you take Comet, and Chelsea, you take Dancer. The dogs know the course, so just keep an eye on them and they'll be fine."

Stacie and Chelsea took their dogs through the agility course. It was a really fun course, with cool tunnels and jumps. The girls were having a great time, but Stacie was still pretty upset with Chelsea.

"Can't you stop doing everything I do? I can't do anything without you tagging along!" Stacie said to Chelsea as her dog jumped over a ball.

"So what? I'm your sister. You're supposed to want me around," replied Chelsea.

"Well, I don't. Not all the time," said Stacie.

"That's just mean!" Chelsea said, feeling a little hurt.

"I just want to be able to do something without you following me! Can't you ever leave me alone?" Stacie yelled.

"Fine! Be alone! See if I care!" Chelsea cried as she stormed off. In front of her, Chelsea could see a cute husky puppy. He was wearing reindeer antlers and was tied to a little sleigh next to a sign that said North Pole. Chelsea walked up to the puppy as he wagged his tail. She could read that on his collar it said Rudy. She climbed into the sleigh and sat down. It was so cool. It was just like she was in Santa's sleigh!

"Now dash away, dash away, dash away all!" Chelsea sang out loud.

In the distance, a squirrel was collecting some nuts. At the sound of Chelsea's cheer, the squirrel got scared and started to run. Rudy saw the squirrel running and began to chase after him. Chelsea was knocked back into the sled. She held tight as the sled rocketed away.

Chelsea sped right past Barbie, Skipper, and Stacie. The three sisters raced after her. When they finally caught up with Chelsea, they were so happy she was okay.

"Chelsea, you can't just take off like that," Barbie said as she tried to catch her breath. "You could have gotten really hurt."

"I didn't take off. Rudy did," Chelsea replied.

"But you were supposed to be in the agility ring with Stacie," Skipper added.

"I was! Until Stacie kicked me out. She told me to go away," Chelsea said.

"I did not!" Stacie insisted.

While Stacie and Chelsea continued to argue, Barbie knelt down next to Rudy and began petting his fluffy fur. Barbie looked into the distance where he was staring. Her

jaw dropped. A herd of real reindeer was grazing near the woods! Barbie quietly got her sisters' attention. They were all amazed.

"Real reindeer. Like the ones we saw this morning," Chelsea whispered so she didn't disturb the reindeer.

"Eight of them. Just like . . ." Skipper said as her thoughts trailed off.

"Yeah, *just* like," said Chelsea with a smile. The reindeer were starting to move. The sisters followed. Soon the girls could see a clearing in the woods where there was a beautiful barn. Next to the barn were a stable and an open corral. The reindeer walked inside the corral and started snacking on bins full of food.

"I guess this is where they live," Skipper said. "But no one is around. There aren't even any houses around here. Who takes care of them?"

As she asked this, Chelsea sneaked into the barn and couldn't believe what she saw. "You guys—you *have* to see this!" Chelsea shouted with glee.

"Chelsea, you shouldn't be in there!" Barbie responded.

"I know, but it looked so cute. Just come

on!" Barbie, Skipper, and Stacie walked toward the barn. Once they were inside, the sisters discovered another surprise. The barn was filled with wrapped presents! There were so many that they practically touched the ceiling.

"Do you know what this is?" Chelsea said with a look of wonder.

"It's a barn and it's not ours," Barbie reminded her sister.

"It's not ours . . . it's *Santa's*!" Chelsea giggled. "Just think about it: eight reindeer, all these presents—it has to be Santa's!"

"Or Christie's. Remember, she said they do that big toy drive every year? Maybe this is where they keep them," Skipper tried to explain.

"But could they really collect this many toys?" Stacie asked.

"Maybe if they worked hard all year?" Barbie added, not believing herself.

"Let's ask Christie and see what she says," Skipper suggested. "Plus, I want to get back someplace warm. I'm freezing."

Chelsea didn't want to leave Santa's workshop, but she was excited to get another ride in the sleigh. She hopped in it.

"Time for another ride, Rudy!" she called.

"How about I pull you instead?" Barbie offered. "It's a long walk, and I don't want you to get dragged off in another squirrel chase," Barbie said as she handed Rudy's leash to Stacie.

Chapter 5

After a while, the girls realized that by following the reindeer, they had gone even farther from the hotel.

"Are we close? We've been walking *forever*," Chelsea complained.

"Not too far," Barbie assured her, though she wasn't quite so sure herself.

"You can't complain. This was all your fault," Stacie said with a hint of anger in her voice.

"This is *your* fault. You wouldn't let me play with you," Chelsea replied.

"You wouldn't stop copying me!" Stacie insisted.

"Come on, cut it out. We all want to get back to . . ." Skipper trailed off as she heard something in the distance. As the girls took a few more steps, they could hear music coming from an old gas station. "Do you guys hear that awesome music? They're rocking out Christmas carols!"

"It's cool," Barbie said.

"Cool? It's sick!" Skipper exclaimed as she ran toward the garage the music was coming from. She stood on her tippy toes and peeked in the window. She saw four guys playing instruments. Skipper knocked on the window to get their attention. The guitar player saw her. The music stopped, and the garage door opened.

Skipper walked inside with a wave. "Hey! Killer sound," she said.

"Thanks! I'm Brian, by the way," the guitar player said.

"Nice to meet you, Brian. You guys are great. Are you online? Where are your videos posted? I totally want to link up

40

to you," Skipper said as she took out her phone.

"Link up to—dude! I know you! P. J. Sherwood, right?" Brian said in disbelief.

Skipper smiled. She couldn't believe she just got recognized! "Wow! Yeah. I mean, Skipper, in real life . . . but yeah! I can't believe you knew that," she said, blushing a little.

"Are you kidding? Your site is, like, *required* viewing. I went there today. You were supposed to be in New York doing a podcast for that new band, but you couldn't get there because of the snow, and—and you ended up *here*!" Brian said. He paused. "And you'd seriously link to our videos?" he asked.

"In a heartbeat! Here, give me the links and I'll put them in my phone," she said.

"Dude, I'd love to, but . . . I mean . . . we don't have any videos," Brian said, a little embarrassed.

"Oh. But you have a website, right? Who does your vocals?" Skipper asked.

"No one," Brian admitted. "That's kind of our big problem. We play pretty great, but we don't have a website or MP3s or anything 'cause we don't have a lead singer. We're just kind of jamming until we find one," he explained. "Well, thanks anyway. You have no idea how much I wish I could take you up on the link thing, but . . . you know . . ."

"Yeah, that's a bummer. Good luck, though. You guys are really great!" Skipper said sincerely.

Brian waved to Barbie, Stacie, and Chelsea, and headed back into the garage.

The band started playing again. As the sisters started walking away, Barbie noticed that Skipper looked really bummed out.

"Are you okay?" Barbie asked.

"Yeah, it's just that those guys reminded me of Zoe's band. I'm still upset about losing the chance for them to perform my song live, you know?" Skipper said.

Suddenly, Barbie had a great idea. "Oh! What if . . ." she began to say. But she remembered her promise to Skipper.

Skipper noticed and laughed. "It's killing you not to say it, isn't it? Go ahead before I change my mind," Skipper said with a grin.

"Podcast Brian's band tonight, the same way you were going to do Zoe's! They can even play your song—and you can sing it!" Barbie suggested. "You should put together a Christmas Eve concert at the hotel! I bet Christie would love it. We'll make a stage right outside, we can serve Christie's amazing hot cocoa as people come in—"

"Hold up," Skipper interrupted. "If I'm going to do this, *I* want to do it. I don't want it to be a Barbie thing."

"Deal. If that's what you want, I'll totally keep out of it," Barbie promised.

Skipper thought for a moment. "You really think I could pull it off?"

"I know you can," Barbie said with a reassuring smile.

And with that, Skipper turned to race back to the garage and tell the band about the concert!

Chapter 6

Once they were back at the hotel, Skipper had a lot of planning to do. The sisters and the guys from the band were standing outside the hotel. Skipper was explaining the concert idea to Christie.

"A Christmas Eve concert is a *great* idea!" Christie said. "I know just who to call to make sure everyone knows about it."

"Excellent. The band and I will need a place to rehearse. Could we rehearse in the hotel?" Skipper asked.

"Yes. You can play in the basement. And you can set up a stage out here for the show. We can put out risers with blankets and refreshment tables. Whatever you need, just ask the Elifs and me and we'll help!" Christie said.

"Thanks!" Skipper said.

"I want to help, too," Stacie chimed in.

"Me too," Chelsea added. "What can we do?"

"I have an idea," Christie said with a wink to Skipper. "Maybe you could help with the opening act. You could do an animal show with the shelter dogs. A couple of them still need to be adopted, and with the huge turnout I know you'll have, it will be a great way to showcase them."

"Yes! That's an excellent idea!" Skipper said.

"Just me, or both of us together?" Stacie asked.

"Both of you together. Think you can handle that?" Skipper asked.

"Yeah!" Chelsea cheered.

"Yeah, I can handle it," Stacie said as she rolled her eyes.

"What are you going to do for the show, Barbie?" Chelsea asked.

Barbie started to answer Chelsea but then stopped. She wasn't sure how involved Skipper wanted her to be in the show.

"*You* will make popcorn-and-cranberry strings," Skipper said with a big smile. "Decorations totally set the scene!"

Barbie smiled back at her sister and said, "If that's where you need me, I'm all over it." Then Barbie walked away and headed inside the inn.

"Okay, so here's what we're going to do. . . ." Skipper started.

After creating a huge cranberry-and-popcorn string, Barbie wondered if everything was going according to plan for Skipper. She went outside to take a peek.

A few minutes later, Barbie was looking at a disaster zone. The stage was in large pieces, with several different colored curtains lying out. Risers were pointing in completely different directions. Half-painted signs were all over the ground.

"Barbie! I'm so glad you're here!" Christie said as she approached Barbie.

"What's going on? Isn't the show in just two hours?" Barbie asked.

"Yes! But Skipper hasn't told us where

she wants the stage, or what color curtains to use, or—"

"But you don't need her for all that, right? You know this spot. Just do what you think is best," Barbie advised.

"I would, but Skipper won't let us. She gave us distinct orders not to make a single decision without her," Christie said.

"Really?" Barbie asked as she turned her head to listen to an argument going on near the dog area. She walked over to Stacie and Chelsea.

"Barbie! Stacie's being super mean!" Chelsea whined.

"I'm not! I just think it's better if we each do our own animal acts with the dogs. I want to be the Stupendous Stacie!" Stacie said.

"And I want to be her lovely assistant," Chelsea added.

"I don't want a lovely assistant. I want to do my own thing. You can, too. You can be Chillin'-it Chelsea or Charming Chelsea," Stacie suggested.

"Those are dumb. I want to do the show with you," Chelsea said as she and Stacie turned to Barbie.

"Um, I guess it's really up to Skipper," Barbie said, not knowing what to do. Suddenly, Barbie heard another noise in the distance.

"*Arrrgghhh!*" Skipper groaned. She was in the middle of the pieces of the set. Christie was trying to help her. The sisters went over to help, too.

"I don't know! It's too much to think about! And I still have to rehearse and set up the podcast and decide on outfits. . . ." Skipper trailed off.

"It's okay," Christie said, trying to calm Skipper. "We can decide this stuff for you. Let us figure it out."

"No! I need to do it myself like Barbie. She always—" Just then Skipper saw Barbie. She tried to get herself together and act like she had everything under control. "Oh. Hi, Barbie," she said in a calm voice.

Chelsea raced over to Skipper. "What do you like better, two animal acts or one with a lovely assistant? I think one is better, but Stacie won't let me do it and I need you to tell her how important it is because I—"

"What? Not now, Chelsea," Skipper said with annoyance.

"But you need to tell her now or it'll get too late and—"

"Not now! Seriously, just stop!" Skipper yelled.

"See? Now Skipper's mad at you, too. You are in everybody's way," Stacie said to Chelsea.

"I am not! I'll prove it to you!" Chelsea said as she stormed off.

Stacie rolled her eyes. "You don't have to be a baby about it," she said as she went back toward the dogs.

"Um, Skipper, can I talk to you for a minute?" Barbie asked gently.

"Sure," Skipper replied as she walked with Barbie. "This must look like kind of a mess to you. I mean, you do stuff like this by yourself all the time, and it's always great. I'll get it right, though. I will."

"Skipper, I never do anything like this by myself," Barbie said.

"You do! I've seen you! You've put on plays, and hosted block parties, and what about that fashion show you did in Paris for Aunt Millie?" replied Skipper.

"I didn't do any of those things by myself," Barbie explained. "Tons of people helped me. I couldn't have done it without them."

"Really? I never knew that. From the

outside it looks like you can do anything," Skipper said. "It's kind of hard to measure up to sometimes."

"Measure up to?" Barbie couldn't believe what she was hearing. "Skipper, I think you're *amazing*! Look at what happened with Brian—he was in awe of you and your site, and that's something you put together all on your own."

"I guess," Skipper said quietly.

"It's true! You don't have to compare yourself to me or anyone else. You're incredible just the way you are," Barbie assured her sister.

"Thanks," Skipper said with a huge smile. Suddenly, Barbie and Skipper heard really loud barking. The dogs were getting out of control. They were chasing a family of squirrels around the set! While they were running after the squirrels, the dogs ripped the curtains on the stage and knocked over the risers. "It's almost time for the show and everything is ruined," Skipper said with tears in her eyes. She turned to Stacie and said, "I thought you and Chelsea were watching the dogs."

"But we were!" Stacie replied. "Then Chelsea pouted off the way she does."

"Wait a minute," Barbie interrupted. "Pouted off? Pouted off where?" Barbie, Skipper, and Stacie looked around. No one saw Chelsea. The three sisters looked at one another. They called to Christie to ask if she had seen her.

"She couldn't have gone far," Christie said calmly. "We can fan out and look."

Then Stacie noticed something in the snow. "Look, there are sleigh tracks over here. Has anyone seen Rudy, the husky puppy?"

"She must have had him pull her away in the sleigh. And it's getting dark!" Skipper said, getting more concerned.

"She's out there somewhere all by herself on Christmas Eve. I have to go find her," Barbie said.

"*We* have to go find her," Skipper added. "We're *sisters*. We work together. We always should."

Stacie stepped closer to her sisters. "Right. I'm in, too."

Chapter 7

It began to snow as the sisters followed the sleigh tracks. They had been calling Chelsea's name for a long time, but they still couldn't find her. With the snowfall starting to get heavier, the sleigh tracks started to disappear.

"Where do we go now?" Skipper asked her sisters.

Barbie thought for a moment. "Aside from the hotel, I can only think of one

place she'd want to go," Barbie explained as she headed farther from the hotel.

Barbie had led her sisters to the stables where they saw the reindeer earlier in the day. The sisters went into the stables, calling Chelsea's name. Barbie found her curled up fast asleep next to Rudy. The sleigh was sitting outside the stall. Chelsea thought she had heard someone calling her name as she woke up.

"Barbie?" she called as she wiped the sleep out of her tired eyes. "Hi, guys!" she said as she saw her sisters. Barbie, Skipper, and Stacie raced over to Chelsea and gave her a huge group hug. Chelsea was laughing."You're crushing me!" She giggled.

"What were you doing here?" Barbie asked.

"I wanted to see the reindeer. And all eight of them were here. They played with me and Rudy, and let me pet them, and . . . I guess I fell asleep, 'cause that's all I remember," Chelsea explained.

"But why did you run away?" Skipper asked.

"I didn't run away. Stacie said I was in

everyone's way, and you were mad at me. So I thought you'd be happier if I left you alone," Chelsea explained.

"Oh, Chelsea, that's not true! You're my sister. I love having you around!" Skipper said.

"Me too," Stacie admitted. "Even when I don't like having you around, I love having you around."

"Really?" Chelsea asked with a smile on her face. She threw her arms around Stacie, and Skipper hugged both of them.

"I want in, too!" Barbie called as they all shared another group hug.

"I was thinking, one animal act is probably better than two. And I could definitely use a lovely assistant," Stacie said to Chelsea.

"You mean it?" Chelsea asked.

"She *would* mean it—if there was going to be a show," Skipper said as she looked at her watch. "It's supposed to start in an hour, but we don't even have a stage. There's no way we could be ready in time."

"I'm so sorry, Skipper. It was your big Christmas Eve show, with a great new band playing your song, and now . . . I feel awful. I know it meant everything to you," Barbie said.

"You must feel like your whole Christmas is ruined," Stacie added.

"Are you kidding? I'm with the three of you. As long as we're together, it's the perfect Christmas," Skipper explained.

"So we are having a perfect Christmas!" Chelsea said excitedly. "Oh—and I know what can make it even more perfect! You have to come play with the reindeer! Come on!" Chelsea called as she headed out of the stables. The three sisters followed. It had stopped snowing outside. Chelsea searched and searched, but there were no reindeer to be found. All was quiet until suddenly a noise that sounded like sleigh bells rang through the air. And then the girls heard a cheerful "Ho-Ho-Ho!" Their eyes opened wide in amazement.

"Did you guys hear that?" Barbie asked her sisters.

"Was it . . ." Chelsea's voice trailed off.

"Those weren't here a minute ago, were they?" Skipper asked as she pointed to the ground. There were sleigh tracks, much bigger than the ones Chelsea's sleigh made in the snow.

"Santa! Let's follow them," Chelsea said as she started to run after the path of the tracks. Suddenly, the tracks stopped.

"That's weird. The tracks just stop. Almost like—" Barbie said.

"—like the sleigh took off into the air," Chelsea finished Barbie's thought. All the sisters looked up in the sky, but they did not see a sleigh.

"Um, you guys, come look," Stacie called. The other sisters stopped gazing upward to see that Stacie was at the open barn door, looking inside with amazement. They joined her, and together they all stepped inside the barn. All the presents that had filled the barn to the ceiling were gone.

"Wow!" Barbie gasped.

"Santa took them!" Chelsea cheered as she jumped up and down with excitement. "And he left us a present—the perfect place to do Skipper's show!" The girls looked further into the barn and could see a stage, a curtain, amazing lighting, seating, and tables for refreshments. It was Christmas magic!

"And look—our stockings!" Stacie cheered as she pointed to their stockings filled with presents hanging over a fireplace. It was too incredible to believe.

"Ho! Ho! Ho! What a great place for a show!" a woman's voice came from the door. It was Christie.

"Hey, Chelsea! Glad you're okay," Christie said as she hugged Chelsea. Then she turned to Skipper. "Do you love it?"

"I do, but . . . doesn't it belong to someone? I mean, it's perfect, but we can't just use it . . . can we?" Skipper asked.

"It belongs to my family, and I insist you use it. Besides, I already made a bunch of calls. There's a whole audience on its way," Christie said.

"You already . . . but how did you know?" Skipper asked.

"My uncle called me, after he picked up all the presents in here. He said it would be the perfect spot," Christie explained.

"Your uncle picked up all the presents here by himself? Is that even possible?" Stacie asked, not knowing what to believe.

"My uncle does his best work on Christmas Eve. It's amazing what he can accomplish," Christie answered.

"But how did he even know we needed a place for the show? And how did he do all this . . . ?" Skipper's voice trailed off. She realized the only possible answer. She looked at Christie, who smiled knowingly back at her.

"So, what do you think, Skipper? There's forty-five minutes left until showtime. Do you think you can do it?" Christie asked.

"No. No way," Skipper said sadly. Then

she smiled and added, "Not without lots and lots of help. Will you guys help me?"

"We'd love to," Barbie said with a smile. And with that, Christie and the sisters got to work. There was a lot to do before the show!

Chapter 8

It was minutes before the show and the last few audience members were taking their seats. The barn was packed! Christie was greeting people at the door and leading them to the only open seats left. Barbie was working the concession stand. She had just poured a hot chocolate for a happy customer. She smiled as she looked out on the packed house. She was so excited for her sisters.

"Can you take over for a moment?" she asked Christie.

"Of course!" Christie replied.

Barbie slipped behind the curtain and headed backstage. She saw Skipper standing with the band and Chelsea and Stacie playing with the dogs. "Hey, how are you feeling?" she asked her sisters.

"Really good. Thanks to you guys. I never could have pulled this off without you. Now here I am, doing almost the exact thing I wanted to do in New York, but it's even better here because you're all a part of it, too," Skipper said.

Chelsea couldn't agree more. "My Christmas is better here, too. I'm still part of an animal show, but I get to do it with Stacie."

"And I got to sled and play in the snow, but with all of you," Stacie added.

"I got what I wanted, too. I'm backstage at a once-in-a-lifetime show," Barbie said with a smile.

Christie popped her head backstage. "It's time!" she cheered.

"Break a leg," said Barbie as she went to hug her sisters. Then she went with Christie to slip back out into the audience. The house lights dimmed and the curtain opened. Skipper walked out onstage to the crowd applauding.

Skipper nodded to the band. They started playing the song Skipper wrote and she totally rocked the vocals. During the song, Stacie and Chelsea brought out nine shelter dogs dressed up in Christmas outfits. The audience loved it. As the dogs finished performing onstage, Chelsea and Stacie bowed. Skipper signaled to the band to slow down the beat and she spoke into the microphone.

"You know, there's no way I can finish this song without some help. I'd like three very special people to join me: my sisters, Barbie, Stacie, and Chelsea!" Skipper cheered as her sisters came onto the stage. "Thanks to my sisters I learned that the

perfect Christmas can happen anywhere, as long as you're sharing the joy of the season with the people you love. Everyone in this town has been incredibly good to us, and I hope by sharing our love and happiness, we're a part of your perfect Christmas, just like you're all a part of ours."

And with that, the four sisters sang the final chorus in beautiful harmony. As it ended, the audience exploded with applause and gave the sisters a standing ovation. The sisters bowed. Then Skipper pointed to the band to make sure they got the special attention they deserved as well.

Even though the lights were bright, the sisters could see that Christie was leading someone down the main aisle toward the stage. Then they realized who the special guest was.

"Aunt Millie?!" Barbie shouted in disbelief.

"Merry Christmas, girls!" Aunt Millie cheered as the sisters rushed down from the stage to give their aunt a huge hug.

"I can't believe you're here!" Barbie said.

"Oh, yes! It wasn't easy, though. The storm shifted and only a few planes took off. I think I sprained my ear from all the time I spent on the phone trying to get a seat! I had to promise almost everyone at the airline a custom-made outfit from my newest fashion line," Aunt Millie explained.

"You did that for us?" Stacie asked.

"Honey, I came all the way from Paris to New York to see my favorite girls. What's a few more miles to Minnesota?" Aunt Millie turned to Skipper. "You were brilliant, darling. You all were brilliant."

"Thanks, Aunt Millie," Skipper said.

"It really is the perfect Christmas," added Chelsea.

Just then the group heard excited barking coming from outside. Chelsea headed toward it to see what was going on. She stopped in the doorway and called out in amazement, "You guys! You have to come see this! Everyone, come look!"

Barbie and her family went outside, their faces glowing with light. They all smiled. Soon the audience was outside as well.

"It's so beautiful," said Stacie. They were all gazing at a very large evergreen outside the barn. The tree was now magically decorated to be a perfectly beautiful Christmas tree.

"It's incredible, but how?" Aunt Millie asked.

"It's Christmas magic, Aunt Millie!" Chelsea explained.

Everyone was quiet as they admired the tree. Barbie was so thankful to have all of her loved ones around her. She looked at her family and the amazing people who had made their Christmas extra special. Even though they couldn't make it to New York, the sisters had the perfect Christmas after all.

Spend the Holidays with Barbie

Coming to DVD this Holiday Season!

Celebrate the Holidays with Barbie™ and her Sisters in their All-New Movie!

You Can Add These DVD Treats to Your Holiday Wish List!

All-New Barbie Movie Now Available on DVD!